Ghosts

of the

Wabash River

Dedicated to
all the folks along
the Wabash River
who have to
put up with those
who haven't really gone
away...even after
they've gone away.

Table of Contents

The reader should understand that we were able to obtain some of these stories only if we promised to obscure some of the actual identity of persons and/or property. This required us to occasionally use fictitious names. In such cases, the names of the people and/or the places are not to be confused with actual places or actual persons living or dead.

Preface

So, why are there so many spooks that hang out along the Wabash River?

Maybe ghosts simply enjoy that beautiful river as much as the rest of us do.

This book tells us about a number of these spooks and how they end up pestering perfectly law-abiding folks who still live on this side of that great divide into eternity.

A Good Friend

The allegations of how a blind person will find his other senses sharpened is not an old wives' tale. That often happens.

There are schools of thought about how and why that happens. This story doesn't address the hows and the whys of that situation. It only relates an incident that happened in Clinton back in the 1950s.

This is a story about a blind fellow who lived in a house there in town. The fellow lived alone for many years in his modest home in the shadow of a water tower. A second version of this tale has it that his neighbor was the beginnings of a sizable steel-framed building that was never finished, the work having come to an end when all the building consisted of was the skeleton of some huge girders.

The accounts of this story agree that the blind fellow was in the practice of sitting near the picture window that pretty much faced south.

Apparently that spot was a favorite place for the man. While he couldn't enjoy the view, his place near the picture window allowed some of the outside noises to enter the house. In addition, the man could enjoy the feel of sunshine on his legs as he'd sit there on a sunny winter day.

We don't know the man's name, so we'll simply call him John Smith for the sake of convenience.

Most of the time John would keep track of the time by means of an old-fashioned clock with the glass removed. He could feel around on the face of that clock, determine the location of the hands and thus learn the time.

But, when it was sunny, John didn't have to feel around on that clock. He'd know it was noon when one of the legs of that water tower would cast a shadow on John's own legs.

John would pick up on the small dropping of the temperature caused by the shadow of that leg of the water tower. That drop in temperature was John's signal that it was time to go out into the kitchen and hustle up his lunch.

Thus life went on for John Smith, a life of darkness and driven by routine and habit. But routine can be of comfort when one is burdened by the handicap of loss of vision. It was a lifestyle imposed on John due to his circumstances, but he got along just fine.

And John's little house there in Clinton was just right for him. He had little space, but needed little space. He had several friends and a shirttail relative who would drop in on him from time to time to see how he was getting along, and to see if he needed anything. One of the fellows would mow John's lawn, another would tidy the outside up, and others would do other little chores, chores that John found to be extremely difficult or impossible. John was fortunate in having friends who would make life easier for him than it would have been otherwise. He felt kind of bad about having to depend on the kindness of others, but the others would brush aside any suggestions that they were doing any more than what was expected of them as being decent citizens.

Things went on in this vein for a long time, then things changed a little. A friend of John's learned about a blind man who didn't want to live in an institution of any kind, and no resources to buy the services of others. This friend of John's thought those two would make a good fit and got the two of them together. We don't know the name of this second blind fellow either, so again, we'll give him a name as a matter of convenience. We'll call him Joe Blow.

What ended up happening was that Joe moved in with John there in John's house. It took a little accommodation to make it all happen, but John was more than happy to make those compromises in order to help this fellow. John figured that this was a way he could repay someone for all the help that he had gotten through the years.

This turned out to be a really good deal for both John and Joe. It provided Joe with exactly what he needed: a place to live that was a real home and not an institution of some sort.

And, not only did it give John an opportunity to be of help to someone else, but it also provided him with the companionship he sorely needed.

It certainly didn't take long for the two of them to become good friends. They both enjoyed each other's company and got along just fine. The two of them had a lot in common in terms of interests, and spent countless hours just visiting. And it turned out that they were both avid chess players and card games of all kinds. John had a deck of cards notched in such a manner that one could read the card simply by feeling the notches on the sides of each card. Playing chess was no problem either. The squares were separated by tiny raised walls so the fellows could keep track of where their chessmen were. It took a lot of time, feeling those chessmen to play a game, but time was one commodity they both had in abundance, so that worked well.

Joe had virtually no resources, but John had fallen into some money and had enough to pay the bills, buy the groceries and provide for the modest needs of two fellows getting kind of long in the tooth.

Joe was endlessly grateful for what his new friend and benefactor had done for him, and would often try to convey to John how very, very much he appreciated the help he got, and it was kind of frustrating to know he couldn't pay John back for all that. Furthermore, he had no anticipation of ever being able to do so.

John would airily dismiss such talk, explaining how he himself had been the beneficiary of the kindness of others, and how he simply figured he was keeping the cycle of kindness going on around. He also countered such talk by Joe, explaining to Joe how much he appreciated having Joe's company, so it was a win-win situation. John had no anticipation, either, that Joe would ever be able to repay him for the expenses that John had to pick up to make the whole thing happen. But, he didn't care about that, and was perfectly happy to do what he could to help his new friend.

It was in 1958 that Joe died. Apparently it was simply old age. He went to sleep one night and never woke up.

John found himself alone again. He missed his friend and missed their many conversations. He missed the card games they'd play and their contests in games of chess.

The loss of Joe was just plain a bummer situation for John. But he had to make compromises with life before and this was simply another one to make. Because his routine never had been seriously disturbed by the coming of Joe, John found it easy to slip back into his old routine.

It was on a sunny winter day when John was seated at his spot there by the picture window. It was a peaceful kind of day, a lazy kind of day, and John had no reason to know that a mile down the highway events were getting lined up to completely change his life. That was a busy road and there were already plans on the drawing boards to reroute parts of that highway there in Clinton to get it away from so many houses, and to make it more efficiently find its way through Clinton. But on this sunny winter day, those were only plans and fate was putting events together that would change everything.

John was fully aware of that highway just outside his home. He was aware of the fact that the highway took a turn right there near his house. That turn was a mean little turn, deceptive in how slow or fast was appropriate to negotiate it.

He was sitting there in his favorite spot when he felt that old familiar sudden cooling of his pants leg, telling him that the shadow of the water tower had entered the window, and that it was time to go out to the kitchen to get some lunch put together. This was kind of confusing to John, since he had no idea it had gotten that late. He reached over to his clock to feel the hands so he could be assured it was time for lunch. The hands on that clock indicated that it wasn't even 10:30 yet.

By this time that huge semi had cut that mile's distance in half. It was now just half a mile from John's house.

Investigations of the events of that day revealed that the alcohol count of the driver's blood was well over the legal limit. That conspired with an icy spot on the highway and the deceptiveness of that mean little curve.

But the events of importance of that day had still not arrived by the time John turned to go out into the kitchen to check the time with a second clock he had out there on the table. John was unaware of what was going to be happening in a matter of seconds.

The kitchen was added on to the main house years earlier, so it was kind of set off from the main portion. John had just gotten to the table and was reaching for his clock so he could solve the question as to what time it was.

Suddenly the entire house, except for the kitchen, erupted in a cloud of dust, flying boards and shredded furniture. Suddenly, instead of the kitchen having been "added to" the rest of the house, the rest of the house became "subtracted from" the kitchen.

That semi had left the highway and reduced the main portion of that modest house to a pile of rubble, still obscured in a cloud of plaster dust. John, of course, didn't see that dust. All he knew was that he was overcome by a deafening roar and the kitchen was filled with the cold winter air that was supposed to stay outside. But, the outside came into that kitchen with the disappearance of the rest of the house.

That semi, plowing into that little house at a high speed left it looking like a strewn toy. There remained no piece taller than the wheels of the semi, now laying on its side in the yard.

John's routine was such that he simply never would have been out in that kitchen at 10:30 in the morning. What had sent him out there was the need to find out what the time was. The shadow that crossed his lap, that shadow of the leg of the water tower had told him it was noon, yet his clock out there on the window sill said it was only 10:30.

The shadow of the leg of the water tower had a full hour and a half yet before it would be where it would have shone through that window.

How could all this be? Shadows show up when they are supposed to, not an hour and a half earlier. John knew how it could be. He knew as he stood out in the yard, watched over by a policeman. He knew why that shadow had crossed his legs an hour and a half early. He knew that Joe had found a way to give John a hand as payment for the huge favor that John had done for him.

John Smith found a new house to live in, and soon found a favorite spot in that new house where he could enjoy the feeling of sunshine on his legs on sunny winter days. And he found new friends, but never one as true a friend as Joe had been to him.

Joe, or at least Joe's ghost, saved his life, and John would never forget that.

The Entrepreneur

One of the luckiest guys in the world was Estes Franklin. Estes lived out in the country, south of Terre Haute.

Estes got caught right up 'long side the head, not once, but twice by Lady Luck. Yes, Lady Luck hit him twice, one time right after the other.

Estes' first stroke of good luck was in the form of a letter from a lawyer. The letter was in the nature of an announcement that Estes was the sole beneficiary of an uncle's will. The man's estate was all wrapped up in a trust, and the trust was left to Estes.

Estes hardly remembered that uncle, but he ended up a rich man because of him..........rich to the tune of three million dollars!

News of that letter from that lawyer set the tongues to wagging. They wagged all the way from the beauty parlor to the pool hall. It became the talk of folks up at the country club as well as the guys over at Tom's Tattoos.

It wasn't too often that folks from south of Terre Haute could lay claim to the fact that they knew a person who fell into almost three million dollars. It was all pretty exciting.

Then, Lady Luck caught ole Estes again. This was an even better deal. This was better than the almost three million dollars.

This second stroke of luck was the information that the inheritance wasn't going to be given to Estes all at once. It wasn't going to be doled out over a thirty-five year span of time.

Now that second stroke of good luck didn't get all the attention that the first one did, but it was the better deal of the two. Estes might not have known much about his uncle, but Uncle surely must have had Estes' number.

Estes Franklin could not wait to move up the social ladder from an ineffective mechanic to something a whole lot fancier. That inheritance was going to allow Estes to become an entrepreneur. He had no idea in the world of how to spell that, but he was going to be one.

Yep, the arrival of that first check from that trust turned Estes from an ugly duckling into a swan............from a nobody to a real live businessman.

Without even a twinge of remorse, Estes got rid of his automotive repair tools. He never did really understand how cars worked, and that might have had something to do with how infrequently people would hire him to fix theirs.

Estes' first problem was to figure out what he could do to be an entrepreneur. He decided the answer to that was to get into the ice business. He had noticed that more meals were being catered. That had to take a lot of ice. Another thing he had heard about was how folks were getting into ice sculpture. That sounded like a thing that would need a bunch of ice. He just figured that the ice business was a coming thing and he could use that to parlay his yearly take from that inheritance into lots of money.

A nice thing about the ice business was that he could do it part time and get the machinery together to get into business by fall. That way he could run his ice business through the winter

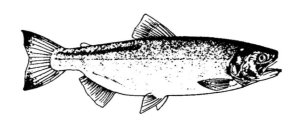

and it wouldn't interfere with his fishing any. That fishing took a lot of his time in the summer, so he figured he could devote his winters to his new business.

The whole prospect of getting in the entrepreneur business was pretty exciting, and Estes used all of that first year's income from that inheritance to make it happen. And, of course, he had to commit to a couple of loans to get the whole thing ready to go by the onset of winter.

We won't go into all the details, but the ice business wasn't what Estes thought it was going to be. He pretty much dismissed suggestions that it was summer business more than a winter one. He figured that folks who talked that way were just jealous of his being able to run a business and do a bunch of fishing down at the Wabash, too.

Estes had plenty of time to mull that whole issue over because it took him two more yearly checks to get shed of those loans he had to take out. Entrepreneuring had to take a two-year delay.

He put that two year's recess from being a businessman to good use. He wanted to come up with a marketing plan that would really wow 'em.

It was at the funeral of a friend of Estes' that led him to the original idea for a different business, a business that would really work. The more he thought of the idea, the better it sounded.

Estes was shocked when he learned about the costs of a funeral. He saw how those expenses worked a real hardship on his friend's parents. He was privy to the breakdown of the cost of that funeral, and realized that the cost of the casket was a major part of the whole bill.

Estes' marketing instincts kicked in and he realized there was a huge potential for rental caskets........caskets you could just rent instead of having to lay out all that money to buy one. Families wouldn't be burdened with the oppressive cost of the casket. It'd be far easier for people to rent a casket, just so much a month, or year, or whatever.

The nice thing about being in the casket rental business was that there wouldn't be any foolishness about 12 easy payments, or "only 36 payments." Those rental payments would go on forever...............forever as in ETERNITY.

Estes figured he could set the rent pretty low. He wouldn't have to lean real heavy for each monthly rental. With the deal going on forever, it would be an attractive deal for Estes.

This time Estes didn't allow himself to be timid.

He bought the full line, all the way from some cheap painted jobs up through the solid mahogany ones, complete with heavy brass handles. On those fancy jobs, there were even some clumps of brass flowers and leaves adorning each corner of the casket.

Those things were pretty pricey, but Estes figured he had such a hot thing going that he'd recoup his costs, and then some in no time at all. After all, forever is a long, long time.

No matter how he figured it, no matter how he penciled it out, he couldn't find a single flaw in the idea, and he could hardly wait to get things going.

Since he wasn't going to allow himself to be timid in this new enterprise, he found it useful to not only spend his fourth annual inheritance check, but to commit to three or four more years with loans to cover all his costs. But, it took a lot of money to get in the casket rental business. There was all that money for the caskets, the need to get some equipment to move 'em around and the need for a building large enough for both an office and warehouse/showroom.

Estes was glad to see a number of local business folks confirm the wisdom of what he was up to. These people were some of the businesses he dealt with, ranging all the way from the realtor to the lumberyard and the contractors. It made him feel good to know that these folks saw the dream, and urged him on.

The casket rental business turned out to be a tad different than what Estes thought it was going to be, but since this is a book of ghost stories, we'll cut out a lot of this pre-ghost stuff and get right on to how Estes got to be a ghost, and what he did.

There were people who insisted that Estes slamming into that old cottonwood tree at over ninety miles an hour probably would have happened even is his casket business hadn't turned south.

Maybe so, or maybe not. Whatever, the cottonwood tree thing did happen, and Estes shucked those mortal coils.

It didn't take long after the funeral (with a real fancy casket) before Estes' ghost showed up for the first time.

Now, you have to understand that Estes, in the flesh, had been a fairly decent sort of upright citizen. He didn't take up, as far as anyone knew, the practice of window peeping until he did so as a ghost.

Window peeping is pretty much a nasty sort of thing to get into, but Estes did it..........or, at least, his ghost did.

Estes' ghost probably should have gone to some other town to do his window peeping, but he didn't. He did it right there in Terre Haute, and folks were familiar enough with Estes they picked up on who was doing that window peeping just pretty quickly.

When it first got out that they had 'em a window peeper right there in Terre Haute, and it was none other than Estes Franklin, folks got pretty irate. There were any number of calls to the sheriff's office to do whatever it took to put an end to that practice.

The citizens figured that Estes, being almost a three millionaire, shouldn't get him any special attention. Well, more like a two millionaire since that estate had eroded a bit from those businesses. They figured a window peeper was a window peeper, and they wanted it stopped.

That righteous demand for justice lost some of its steam when folks got to realizing that Estes' ghost wasn't a general purpose window peeper. He specialized. He confined his window peeping to folks' garages.

There not being a whole lot of people running around in their garages in their birthday suits, all that made Estes' window peeping less objectionable than it might have been otherwise.

Apparently Estes' inclination for dead-end projects and lost causes spilled over into his ghost messing up the window peeping project.

It wouldn't have taken a whole lot of smarts to recognize it as kind of pointless to window peep into people's garages.

Maybe Estes' ghost was buying advice from whoever Estes had bought it from. Window peeping into garages seems to rank right up there with renting caskets.

Under the Bleachers

Back in the 1940s, the Friday evening movies were a huge part of life in Smalltown, USA.

And a super attractive part of the Friday evening movies was the fact that they were free. Well, they were free to the populace. They were actually possible due to the generosity of the local merchants since they offered an opportunity for the local businesses to advertise. When a movie is preceded by an exhortation to "Eat at Joe's," that's a good deal for Joe when virtually everybody in town was there to read that.

Those circumstances there at Grayville, Illinois, were like in any other small town, and those Friday night movies were popular with merchants and shoppers alike. Some towns had a screen to show these movies on, and some simply used the side of a building as the screen, and would set up bleachers of planks on stands to provide the seating facilities.

For those towns with a permanent set of bleachers, life was a little easier on the local city employees, but there was a down side to permanent bleachers. And that was that the ground under the bleachers would become beds of paper napkins, pop bottles, wads of chewing gum and other such unattractive things.

The movies were chosen to be titles that would be of interest to children, but not to adults. The theory was that, properly managed, the movies would be a way for Mom and Dad to get shed of the kids while they would be off spending money to pay for those "Eat at Joe's" ads.

A book could be written about the social dynamics of those movies. Each of those movies was designed to end with a cliffhanger. The issue at question would be the survivability of the hero (the one in the white hat). Each episode would sadly be determined to be the one in which the hero gets done in. He would find himself in circumstances, in those last few moments of the episode, from which there could not possibly be any escape, and the bad guy (the one in the black hat) would get the ranch/gold/ girl/horse/whatever. This would give the children in town a whole week to argue about if there was any way possible for the hero to escape. The consensus of opinion by the following Friday was that the hero was going to die a horrible death and the black hat would prevail.

During those first few moments of the next episode you could walk an elephant down the aisle, carrying a dozen young ladies in skimpy outfits, each one setting off an M-80 firecracker, and all that not be noticed. Those first few moments would reveal to everybody's surprise and relief that there was a way for Hero to escape after all.

For example, if the hero got tied to a railroad track and a train was approaching, with folks fully expecting that the train would run over him before that band of Indians sneaking up the ravine got to him to do him in..........but the obvious and the inescapable never happened. Our hero would chew the rope that bound him and he'd roll out of harm's way just seconds before the train would roar by, cutting off the threatening Indians in the process. Or, our hero would see a tiny piece of glass on the track, get it up into his teeth where he could hold it in such a manner that it would act as a lens and cause the sun's rays to burn the rope through.

So, that current episode would save hero from certain death in a few seconds, then half an hour later leave him in circumstances that would, for sure, be inescapable, that is until exactly a week later.

Those movies were always grainy, unrealistic and cheap, but they opened up the whole world to those children.

There was another important element to those free Friday night movies. Boys could get in under the bleachers and scurry around under those bleachers pursuing one or the other of two adventures available there.

One of those adventures was the possibility of finding some good stuff. The good stuff consisted of combs, comic books and an occasional coin that would get dropped by the kids up above.

The other adventure that awaited those who would brave that area under the bleachers was the opportunity to peek up girls' dresses if the occupants of those dresses would sit just right.......or just wrong. But the goals of these adventurers could be realized only if the adventurer was willing to put up with the really, really dirty conditions under there. The terrain would consist of combinations of popcorn sacks, mud from the shoes of the farm boys, tobacco juice from neophyte chewers who'd take advantage of the darkness to show off their ability to chew the stuff.........and shortly thereafter, to show off their ability to get sick.

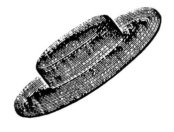

The level of sanitation under those bleachers moved the vast bulk of the mothers to prohibit their offspring from engaging in those under-the-bleachers adventures. And, if the filth under there wasn't bad enough, mothers tended to be a bit narrow-minded about their sons peeking up girls' dresses.

In Grayville, those parental prohibitions about kids ratting around under there put that area off limits to most of the children.

But, not for the Karsey kids. Neither of the elder Karseys would go to town on Friday nights, so those two twelve-year-olds could run amok all they wanted after walking to town, each clutching his dime.

And, if one has the opportunity to run amok, there was nothing amoker than ratting around under those bleachers. So, during that whole summer when the Karsey boys were twelve, anyone who dropped a nickel down there could just about be sure it'd be gone. And the girls knew that if they sat wrong on the bleacher seats, those nasty Karsey twins would be peeking up their dresses.

It was in February of the following year when the Karsey family had their terrible, terrible car wreck. The accident all but wiped the family out. The twins, a younger sister and Mrs. Karsey lost their lives in that accident. Mr. Karsey was the only survivor. Not only did those four die that day, but two others in the other car also lost their lives. It was an horrendous event, one that held the attention of the good people of Grayville for a long time.

By the middle of May when those Friday night movies started up again, the kids had no expectation that the Karsey twins would be pursuing their favorite project again. But they were.

In the shadows and darkness of that area under the bleachers, the kids could hear that familiar shuffling through the junk down there. The most observant of the children would be rewarded with a fleeting glimpse of one or both of the twins. It was always the two of them, still wearing their red and white striped tee-shirts, the same shirts they had always worn back when they were still among the mortals.

So, apparently, just because you are a ghost doesn't mean that a stray nickel now and then loses its appeal. And, nasty ghost boys must enjoy a peek up a girl's dress just as much as their living counterparts.

A number of the girls and even some of the boys in Grayville found those Friday night movies weren't as much fun when ghosts were running around on the loose right under their feet. The blush was off the Friday night movies rose, and the practice barely survived the summer. It didn't even get started the next year.

The Zinc Penny

This whole ghost business gets terribly complicated when a ghost comes back out of the future instead of out of the past.

What happens to time when an event of the future happens? What happens to the concepts of "before and after" when time seems to run backwards?

As the author, I don't even know what end of this story to start on, or if what I have here really ends at all. Perhaps we should start with the events of "modern" times, in the 1940s. Some of these 1940 events predated earlier times in the 1880s, and some came after those events in the 1880s.

Hang in there with me, this can get a bit complicated.

It was in the fall of 1943 when Dr. James Gilroy, recently retired, took his wife with him to visit his childhood home outside of New Harmony. Dr. Gilroy had looked forward to visiting the old home place, then occupied in 1943 by his cousin who had purchased the home from his aunt and uncle, who had been Dr. Gilroy's parents.

The cousin had invited Dr. Gilroy and Mrs. Gilroy to spend a couple days at the house. This was fine with Dr. Gilroy. He planned to wallow in nostalgia as he had grown up in that house, and had lots and lots of memories associated with it. His grandparents had owned the place before his parents and the whole place reeked of history of the Gilroy family.

James Gilroy's memories of the place included recollections of his having explored the cave in the vacant property that adjoined the Gilroy place. He had spent many hours of his childhood in that cave, exploring the many mysteries in there. For all he knew, each of the nooks and crannies had its own eerie history.

In the real world, that mysterious cave wasn't a cave at all. It was simply a large root cellar that had been dug near the back door of a house that had stood on that lot years and years earlier. Those mysterious nooks and crannies were simply what remained of bins created to hold potatoes and apples part way through each winter so the folks in the house could enjoy those things well after the snow had covered the ground.

There were a couple sets of shelves that had survived that still leaned against the dirt wall of that "cave" when Dr. Gilroy had played in it as a youth.

It didn't take long for Dr. Gilroy to make his way to the "cave." He stood there in that root cellar, recalling all the hours he had

spent in that hole in the ground that his imagination had turned into a mysterious cave.

As he stood there, his hand in his pocket chanced upon some stray coins there.

Those coins in his pocket, in that "cave" and under those circumstances, called to mind how he'd hide a coin from himself sometimes as a child. He'd squirrel a penny or a nickel away in some obscure corner, and then find it later. That finding of his coin would delight him to no end. He'd find himself a penny or a nickel richer than he had thought. And, to a kid back in the late 1880s, finding himself a penny or a nickel richer was an occasion of importance and joy.

Smiling in recollection of that youthful practice, he took a few coins from his pocket to go through that again. He stuck one of those coins up on the very top shelf of the one remaining ceiling-high shelf assembly.

So, he did it again. He hid a coin from himself, just as he had done as a child all those years earlier.

The coin was only a penny and Dr. Gilroy had little reservation about leaving a mere penny out in that root cellar. Besides that, it was one of those brand new 1943 pennies that went by the name of a "zinc." Those pennies were minted in 1943 in order to save on copper. Copper was a metal that had lots of applications in the war effort, and the zinc pennies were simply a way to save copper. Dr. Gilroy hadn't approved of those new-fangled pennies, and felt that one less "zinc" in his pocket was just fine.

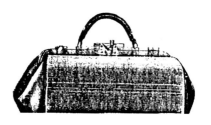

That evening, over coffee and cookies, Dr. Gilroy was sharing the day's activities with Mrs. Gilroy and his cousin and his cousin's wife. He told them about visiting the cave, and how it was a lot smaller than he recalled. He told them about how he had left a zinc there on the top shelf of the sole remaining of the many shelf assemblies that he recalled from his youth. He explained how his leaving that coin was kind of a memento to his childhood practice of hiding a penny or a nickel from himself.

Since Dr. Gilroy's disapproval of the new zinc penny was shared by his cousin, the two of them joked about those fake pennies and the foolishness of the government in general.

All that nostalgic carrying on led Dr. Gilroy's cousin to go up into the attic. He halfway recalled seeing a box of stuff up there that wasn't his and perhaps it belonged to Dr. Gilroy or to his parents.

And, indeed, it proved to be a box of junk that Dr. Gilroy had as a child. It appeared to be mainly some sticks, a couple of which Dr. Gilroy recalled as being ones he had used as toys when he was a kid.

It was apparent to Mrs. Gilroy that if her husband got to ratting around in that box, it could run into several hours of "Oh, here's my..." and shouts of "Good grief, here's this or here's that..." or wondering looks as he would contemplate something that he had no idea why he kept.

Mrs. Gilroy was already tired, as it was late, and had no enthusiasm for the prospect of several hours more of nostalgia. Besides, they were scheduled to leave early in the morning for home, and she wanted to get a good night's sleep.

So, into the car trunk that box went and everyone went on to bed.

The next day, out on the road again, the reality of modern life in 1943 took over the previous few days of wallowing in nostalgia, and Dr. Gilroy lost his appetite to poke around in his memories from the 1880s. The box that he couldn't wait to get into the previous evening got stuck out in the back porch when they got to the house, and life got back to normal.

That is, it got back to normal until about a month later when Dr. Gilroy got run over by a drunk driver. That incident cost him his life.

A lot more months went by before that box on the back porch got looked at again. Mrs. Gilroy was getting ready to sell the house and wanted to get rid of as much junk as she could. She recalled that box from that trip to her husband's cousin's place and regretted having talked her husband out of exploring it. He was past exploring that box now and would never have the experience of going through his childhood goodies.

Wiping away a tear, Mrs. Gilroy opened that box to see if there was anything in it that should be saved or given to either of their children. The contents of that box proved to be of little value. All she found were some notebooks, some sticks, a few little worn-out hand-carved toys and a magnifying glass.

Mrs. Gilroy was about to pitch the whole thing when she ran across a nice leather-bound diary. It proved to be a diary that her husband had kept as an eleven-year-old back in 1888.

While 1888 seems like forever ago now, it wasn't all that long ago back in 1944 when Mrs. Gilroy was ratting through that box.

Without reading much of that diary, Mrs. Gilroy kept the diary and the magnifying glass. The rest of the stuff joined other junk that was piling up; junk that would be hauled away.

It was later that evening when Mrs. Gilroy was looking at that diary closer that she ran into a remarkable thing. There, glued to the page dated 10/12/1888 was a pair of coins. The remarkable thing was that they were both 1943 zinc pennies, almost brand new then in 1944. What in the world were two almost new pennies doing there in a child's diary from 1888?

Reading the page that her husband wrote while still a child only deepened the mystery.

That page went on to tell about how Jimmy Gilroy had found these two coins on the top shelf of one of the shelf assemblies out in the neighbor's cave. It went on to tell that the writer considered the coins to be fakes since they were dated 1943. Not only were the coins carrying a date that was yet 55 years in the future, but they were also white instead of the normal copper.

Jimmy speculated that those two fake coins must have been tokens out of a game or something since they obviously weren't real. They were of an impossible age, and who ever heard of grey pennies?

Mrs. Gilroy was shocked over the whole thing. How could 1943 pennies show up there on a shelf in that root cellar in 1888? Was one of the coins one that her husband had left up on that top shelf? If so, how did it get back into time 55 years? And why were there two instead of just the one her husband had put up there to hide from himself?

Was her husband in 1943 the ghost of himself in 1888? How could a ghost show up before he dies? Where did that second coin come from? Was that the work of her husband's ghost? How could all this be?

Tears of confusion, sadness and fright all but drowned out the message that Mrs. Gilroy had for her son in Terre Haute when she called him then.

Not being able to get a coherent story from his mother, the son, Willard Gilroy, rushed to her home there in Terre Haute to be with his panic-stricken mother.

The whole story of what had happened a few months earlier at Dr. Gilroy's cousin's place, and what Mrs. Gilroy found in that box was gone over time and time again, during the course of the next few days.

No satisfactory answers to Mrs. Gilroy's many questions came of those conversations between Willard and his mother. Nor were answers forthcoming about the many questions that Willard raised while he was there with his mother.

Mrs. Gilroy went home with her son. He came back a couple weekends later, the house got put up for sale and was promptly sold.

There had been enough conversation between Mrs. Gilroy and a neighbor that we know that the diary ended up in a lockbox in town.

We don't know if that diary is still in that lockbox. We don't know how those 1943 zinc pennies showed up in New Harmony in 1888.

We don't even know if this is a ghost story. All we know is that some mighty strange things have happened in this world, and that the Wabash River has had its share of them.

Straight Shootin'

It's hard for us today to relate to some of the issues that early Hoosiers faced when Indiana was still a lonely outpost in our westward expansion. It's hard for us now to properly appreciate how the resources that people had to draw upon back then differed so much from what we need to know, to be and to do in our modern world today.

So it was with Jesse and Sarah Holcomb of frontier Logansport here in Indiana.

Jesse and Sarah lived fairly well in that little valley along the Wabash River where Jesse had put a cabin, a cabin that was to be their home for quite a while.

In that marriage, each of the two had their very specific and well-defined responsibilities. Jesse did the hunting and fishing while Sarah kept the pair fed and clothed. It was daily cooking, cleaning and sewing that occupied her time. Sarah also had responsibility for the garden. All that was a job-sharing formula commonly used on the American frontier.

Jesse's hunting and fishing plus Sarah's garden did a pretty good job of keeping the pair in groceries.

On occasion, a trader wagon would come through. That wagon was the Holcomb's source of flour, seasonings, patent medicines, tools and bullets for Jesse's rifle. Jesse always had some hides to trade for those things.

Each fall, Jesse would literally surround the cabin with firewood in readiness for the long and hard winters they came to expect each year.

The winter of 1888 was a tough one. They had never encountered such a winter before. Game was scarce. The overwhelming snow and the unbelievably cold weather didn't make for an easy winter in '88.

That was also the winter that Sarah lost her husband. He had taken ill and the patent medicines the pair had there in the cabin were no match for whatever befell that frontiersman. Undoubtedly, due to the pain induced by his condition, he went loco. Jesse, in a fit of incoherence, got up from his bed and walked right out into a blizzard that reduced the visibility to almost zero in the day and was impenetrable at night. By the time Sarah woke up and saw what had happened, he was way beyond any efforts she might expend in stopping him or retrieving him. She knew that just a few minutes in that weather was all a man could stand. So after a quarter of an hour had passed, she knew she had lost him. In one mad moment, Sarah had lost her husband and her provider.

That terrible winter had already severely reduced their store of dried meat and the vegetables from their garden that would "keep" part way into the winter.

The one thing they could depend on throughout the winter was all those squirrels that nested and played in the treetops around the cabin. All that Jesse had had to do was to step out on their porch, put his long squirrel rifle to his shoulder and bring down a couple of squirrels and have enough meat for a meal for the two of them.

But now Jesse was gone.

Sarah knew enough about that rifle to get the thing loaded and cocked. She knew how to make it fire. She soon found, however, that that wasn't enough. She knew nothing of the necessity of accommodating the aiming to factor in the blowing of the bullet to one side or the other by the wind, or the drop the bullet would experience as it travels through the air.

Repeated efforts on her part to bring one of those furry creatures down came to nothing. She would line the two sights of the rifle up with the squirrel, pull the trigger and the squirrel would scamper off with an impudent wave of its tail.

She was confused as to why she couldn't hit one of them. She thought she was doing everything right, yet she got none of them.

And, Sarah also knew, from hearing Jesse talk about his hunting, that it didn't do any good to just wound a squirrel in hopes he would die of the wound or fall down onto the ground where she could hit it with a stick. A wounded squirrel was a lost squirrel. They would simply, if injured, pop down the nearest hollow limb and be lost forever.

No matter how many times she tried, she had zero effect on the squirrel population cavorting in those treetops over the cabin.

She knew that things were getting serious and she knew she was in trouble. She was out of food, having eaten that half dried-up potato she found under the stove. She had been reduced to eating the flour, raw, in an effort to keep herself fed.

Sarah found herself getting a little weaker each day as she went from one day to the next without anything to eat. While the inner bark on some of that firewood looked like it was nourishing, and she tried it a number of times, it offered no nourishment to her.

She was finding it a little harder each day to even hold that rifle up in her continued futile efforts to shoot a squirrel. She was in deep trouble and saw no way out of her dilemma. That supply wagon wouldn't be through for weeks. She wasn't sure how many miles it was to the nearest neighbor, and knew she couldn't have made it through that snow much past the edge of the clearing around the cabin.

It was those squirrels that were so frustrating. On sunny days, regardless of the temperature, those playful little critters would come out and chase each other around up there in the treetops. She knew that even just one of them would provide her with enough meat for one meal, with some left over. Yet she couldn't hit them with that rifle and found that attempts to do so simply depleted her stock of bullets.

Sarah's physical condition was such that even those useless trips out to the porch to bang away at those critters would so wear her out that she would have to retreat to her bed for an hour just to recover from the effort. And each time she would regain her strength, she found it to be a bit less than the previous time.

One morning promised to be just one more of a long string of unbelievably cold days. She decided she would make one more trip out on the porch, and then she'd go to her bed and simply stay there. She had never expected to find her life ending that way, but it was obvious that that was what was going to happen.

Out on that porch, Sarah found it impossible to even hold the rifle up with her muscles. She found a niche in the corner log of the cabin, resting the rifle barrel in that little recess.

She rested a bit, having to, due to the efforts to even get outside. Bitterly she thought about how it didn't really make any difference if she was ready for the shot since she couldn't hit one of those things anyway.

Sarah had the two sights of the rifle lined up with the squirrel up there on a limb, and proceeded to squeeze back the trigger.

Just in that last part of a fraction of a second before the rifle would be firing, Sarah felt a decided tug on the rifle, so the very last sight she had down the barrel of the rifle was a patch of blue sky. That's what she ended up aiming at when the sharp crack of the rifle told her the bullet was on its way. She knew it wasn't going to work, she knew she had ended up shooting at a spot in the sky a couple of inches above the limb the squirrel was sitting on, and a good three or four inches to the right of her prey.

She knew in that last instant that she had wasted another bullet, another one of the long string of bullets she had used to shoot holes in the sky.

Sarah had already lowered the rifle down to rest on the handrail of the porch, knowing that everything was all over for her. Her eyes couldn't leave that squirrel up there, a squirrel that could have saved her life had she been able to hit it.

Suddenly the squirrel took one step forward, hesitated but a moment, then plunged to the snow below. She had hit it! She had hit it! Not only had she hit it, but she hit it square enough that it let out not one little wiggle on the way down out of that tree. It fell like a thoroughly dead squirrel, as might it well since that's exactly what it was.

It took all the strength Sarah had to wade out through that snow to gather up her dinner and go inside with it.

While it had been Jesse's job to shoot the game, it had been hers to clean it, readying it for cooking. She knew how to do that little job and did that with muscles weakened through inactivity and lack of nourishment.

In another two minutes she had that critter cut up into chunks and popped into the frying pan there on the stove where she had a fire going to keep warm.

Sarah was beside herself with the joy and excitement of having finally gotten one of those squirrels, and the prospect of a good hot meal in a few minutes.

Unlike what she was accustomed to doing, Sarah ate the entire animal, gnawing each bone as clean as she could to extract every bit of nourishment from that fried squirrel. She let that pan cool off and licked it clean, not letting even one morsel escape her ravenous appetite.

Sarah went to be that night without a restless stomach, growling over having to go to bed without its supper. She was so full and she was so thankful.

That night, Sarah Holcomb slept like she hadn't for a long time. The sleep itself did her a world of good and getting up in the morning was such a wonderful feeling.

Then Sarah got to thinking about her lucky shot, and how she probably couldn't pull that off again that day. Perhaps she had only gotten a reprieve from eventual starvation.

Sobered at that prospect, she went right out onto the porch again, hoping against hope she could repeat the previous day's success. She had thought about that shot the previous day and how lucky she had been, especially since she had let the sights get out of line there at that last minute. She recalled that had felt like a tug of the rifle, but she knew that she had simply let the sights wander in her weakened condition.

Fortunately, the morning broke nice and sunny and those squirrels were out again, chasing each other back and forth from one tree to another, chattering among themselves in spite of the cold weather.

Again, Sarah laid the barrel of that rifle up against the corner of the cabin and lined up the two sights with a squirrel.

She pulled the trigger, but just before the thing went off, she realized that she was going to poke another hole in the sky. This time she felt that tug, but she ended up pointing the rifle above and a few inches to the left of the squirrel.

She didn't even continue looking at the animal up there as she tried to figure out what had caused that little tug on the rifle. As she searched the porch there in front of her, she glanced up just in time to see that squirrel plummeting to the ground.

Surprised, Sarah again struggled out to gather the thing up and take it in to clean and cook it.

While she was hungry this time, she wasn't ravenous, so she took the time to make up a little gravy with some flour and a little oil she had left.

This time she let the squirrel cook slowly, adding some dried leaves she had gotten out of her garden.

That squirrel proved to be as tasty as the one the previous day had. And, miracle of miracles, she ran out of appetite before she ran out of squirrel meat.

As Sarah sat there, she thought again of that little tug she felt on the rifle just before it went off. With a sudden jerk of her head, she, just then, recalled how Jesse had told of how he had to figure for the drop and the windage when he shot game. Those terms "drop" and "windage" had meant nothing to Sarah, but suddenly she realized that Jesse was talking about the need to fire at a place a little bit different than where his target was sitting.

It was then that Sarah also realized what that tug on the end of the rifle had been all about. It was Jesse making a last moment correction so she would hit that squirrel in spite of herself.

Sarah knew that Jesse had come back to help her in the time of her most desperate need.

This whole experience of Sarah's, as well as other of her experiences, was dutifully recorded in her journal, a journal that is in the possession of her great-grandson today.

He shared all that with me when I collared him and told him that I understood he had a ghost story.

This fellow went on to tell me that Sarah stayed two more years in that cabin before catching a ride with a wagon train that came through, headed for the west. She went with them and ended up getting married again and living to be a fairly elderly lady, and one who certainly had a warm spot for her frontiersman husband along the banks of the Wabash.

Up In The Air

It all started when Katie Orwell of West Lafayette developed a back problem while yet in her early thirties. It wasn't an extremely painful problem, just one of those that wouldn't let go.

Katie learned that sleeping in a raised bed and taking hot baths almost solved her entire problem. It was that sleeping in an elevated bed that got the Katie and Ivan Orwell story in this book.

Katie's solution to the need for an elevated bed was simply to plop a single bed mattress down on her side of their double bed, giving her the extra height necessary to help her get in and out of bed. It didn't make the nicest looking bed, but it worked and that's all the Orwells cared about.

That little ploy worked well for many years. She would sleep up there on what she called her "perch," and Ivan laid down there on the regular mattress at the regular bed height. He joked that he didn't want to have to jump off a cliff just to get out of bed in the morning.

Several children, grown and gone, plus a number of new sets of mattresses later, that arrangement was still working well.

The kink in the arrangement came along in December of 1998 when Katie died.

What with the countless details that needed tending to, that now superfluous mattress on the bed got little attention so that "perch" remained on the bed.

Through the years, Ivan had developed the habit of rolling over on his left side, giving Katie what the pair had called "an up in the air" hug.

Years of habit can be hard to break. Ivan found himself reaching up to give Katie her "up in the air" hug from time to time.

Christmas was tough that year. It was Ivan's first Christmas without Katie. The children all came home to be with their father to help him see his way through the season. When one of the girls suggested it was probably time to move that extra mattress, the tears that welled up in Ivan's eyes led her to simply drop the subject.

The warm spot mystery first showed up during those holidays when Ivan was having some difficulty in sleeping and reached over to lay his arm on Katie's mattress. That was simply a matter of habit and he did that sort of thing automatically.

Ivan's sleepy state suddenly evaporated as he realized that the top of that extra mattress was warm. It was the kind of warm that a cold bed will get after someone had been lying on it for some time.

A wide-eyed Ivan felt up and down on that little mattress. Sure enough, there was a Katie-shaped warm spot there on that mattress. A person doesn't sleep with someone else for close to half a century and not be very familiar with that person's size and shape. There was no mistaking it, that was a warm spot that had to be made by Katie.

Mattresses, on a cold December night in an already chilly room, don't just get warm by themselves. That was the work of Katie!

Ivan laid there and realized that Katie had returned to lie there with him. It was at this time that Ivan made the decision that he'd never take that little mattress from his bed.

That next evening, everybody was together, getting in some last minute visiting, since the first of those who would be leaving would be doing so the following morning.

Ivan chose that time to share with his children and his grandchildren his experience of the previous night. He also told them that Katie's mattress was to remain on his bed, regardless of the circumstances.

Ivan got lots of hugs then, along with assurances that his wish would be honored and that the children would see to that.

During the next six years of Ivan's life, he told his children of the occasional reappearance of that warm spot.

Toward the end of that six-year period, one of Ivan's grandchildren was in high school and wanted to "test" his grandfather's silly theory that that spot would get warm on occasion. He didn't call it a silly theory in front of his grandfather, he called it his grandfather's silly theory only when out of earshot of the old fellow.

This young lad's parents weren't real enthused about any kind of "experiment" that the kid would concoct, and only reluctantly asked Ivan about that.

Ivan agreed that if the kid was so all-fired excited about some sort of experiment, he could do it. So, out of that came the idea of putting a recording thermometer up on that mattress of Katie's. It was simply a matter of setting a wire sensor up there, and plugging the machine into the wall. If and when it ever got warm up there, that fact would show up on a piece of graph paper in the machine.

So, the fancy machine came from the high school, got all set up and it's unspoken purpose was to prove that Grandpa had a bit of a loose screw about that bed.

The next appearance of the warm spot escaped Ivan. He apparently just didn't give Katie her "up in the air" hug that night. But, it didn't escape the grandkid's fancy machine. It showed that the temperature went from the high 60s to the low 90s one night for about two hours.

After Ivan died in 2004, the children sold the house, divided up some of the furniture and put the rest of it in storage.

"In storage" consisted of stuffing that remaining furniture into an extra room in their son's house.

That is, the furniture was stuffed in there, except for Katie and Ivan's bed. It was set up, complete with the nightstand, lamp and bedclothes. The bedclothes included the extra mattress there on one side.

That furniture was put in that extra bedroom in 2004. We don't know if a couple of warm spots show up from time to time or not. We don't know if Katie Orwell still gets her "up in the air" hug or not.

The Medicine

Mildred Coopage suffered some sort of knee problem. We have no idea what the problem was, but it was a vexing one.

Mildred, as a child, then as a young adult there in that modest little frame house along the Wabash just outside of Vincennes, suffered a lot from her condition before they finally figured out what would bring her relief.

Back in the middle 1930s, x-rays were fairly well developed, but such things as MRIs and CT scans were simply meaningless collections of letters.

Mildred was only ten years old when her problem started. It was a heavy burden for fate to lay such a problem on a little girl, but it did.

As Mildred became a young lady, the problem intensified and she found every day to be one more painful experience, and each night to be one of sleepless hurting.

While the many visits to the doctors found ways to erode the family's resources, these visits seemed to accomplish nothing else.

One home remedy after the other was tried. Those would vary from one person suggesting her eating certain greens from the woods to a complex combination of heat and light. This latter one involved a machine from the catalog that

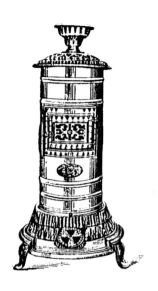

promised immediate and permanent relief from chronic pain, aches and consumptive anxiety.

No one in the family had the slightest idea what consumptive anxiety was, but they sure had a good grip on what aches and pain were. The one thing that all these home cures had in common was that one was just as ineffective as the next.

In a desperate search for relief, Mildred's father tried rubbing a mixture of herbs from the garden and mashed up berries, all worked into a paste by adding it to a horse liniment he had out in the barn.

Strangely enough, that smelly concoction seemed to work better than anything else. It didn't make the hurt all go away, but it did offer a significant measure of relief, enough so Mildred could work through the day pretty well and get some sleep at night.

Every night at bedtime, Mildred's father would rub some of that MMM onto that knee. That gloppy and smelly stuff had earned the name MMM, that meaning Mildred's Magic Mess.

It was Mildred's all right, and certainly was a mess, but the magic was only so-so. But it worked somewhat, and that was what they had.

While Mildred was still at home, she got that treatment there in her bed. After she married, her father continued to come to her place each evening to apply that MMM.

The discovery that the relief that MMM would bring was certainly a welcome one, both to Mildred and others in the family. Every morning Mildred would wake up to find herself smelling like a combination of a pile of freshly-oiled harness and a patch of raspberries right after a rain, for that was what her father made that concoction from, a general purpose horse liniment and some ground up berries and such.

That odor could have been done without, but it was tolerable, given the usefulness of the MMM.

The passage of time and Mildred getting married didn't slow down the performance of that nightly ritual. Mildred's father would show up there at the house each evening and spend an hour rubbing that stuff on her knee. Over the years it involved thousands of hours of work, but it made a lot of difference in Mildred's life.

Mildred's husband would often crack a joke about how it was something of a surprise that the couple ever had any kids, what with his father-in-law being there at her bedside night after night for all that time.

There were several attempts to get her husband and her daughter to learn how to massage that knee, but neither of them ever got the hang of it. Even under her father's careful instructions, the two of them found it useless to try.

As the years passed by, Mildred started to dread the time when her father could no longer do that nightly chore. The few evenings that he had missed gave Mildred a preview of what it was going to be like when he got too old to give her that knee treatment anymore.

It was in early 1957 when the awful day came when Mildred's father's therapy came to an end. The old man went to sleep one night and simply didn't wake up the next morning.

A round of pain killers proved futile. The improved practice of medicine since she was a child didn't bring any new procedures, diagnostic tools or medications that helped her. Mildred tried massaging that knee herself, but she was no better at it than her husband or her daughter had been.

Chronic and severe pain has lots of insidious ways of eroding away ones quality of life way beyond simply having to endure the pain. Mildred developed nervous conditions and even skin rashes, all wrought by the stress of constant and severe pain.

She lost a lot of weight and again found sleep to be all but impossible. It was one of a doctor's observations that the one redeeming thing about the whole situation was that her condition wasn't one that was terminal. Mildred wasn't convinced that was a good thing.

Drugs that would aggressively attack the pain would be of very little benefit, and those drugs promised their own potentials for mischief, so Mildred seemed destined to some awfully terrible years ahead of her. She was, at this time, approaching middle age, and also approaching the end of her rope.

Then suddenly everything changed. She woke up one morning to discover a whole new situation.

She woke up to find that she didn't hurt. Mildred had some difficulty recognizing what it was like to not hurt, but she felt really good.

Mildred laid there, not daring to open her eyes, afraid that the whole thing was a dream, and if it was, it was a dream she didn't want to end. But, it wasn't. It was real. She had slept well and was refreshed. She laid there wondering if her new-found freedom from pain was going to last one minute or one day or what.

Carefully, so as not to break the magic, Mildred slowly pulled off the covers and sat on the edge of the bed. Pulling those covers off released an old familiar odor into the room. It was the odor of a combination of horse liniment and a freshly rained-on raspberry patch.

A childish squeal of delight roused her husband. Getting up to see what was going on, he was greeted by the sight of his wife gleefully dancing around the room, literally radiant with happiness and energy.

The doctors knew no more about why the pain was gone than they had known about where it came from in the first place. They couldn't begin to figure it out. But Mildred could. She knew that her father had come back to do his knee chore with his MMM.

From that morning on, Mildred felt good each day and got some good sleep each night. She didn't feel perfect, but she felt a lot better.........smelled kind of funny, but felt good.

Mildred's husband was thrilled over this new, and certainly welcome, situation. He, too, was convinced that her father had returned to offer relief to his daughter. He had all sorts of clever ideas about how he could lay awake and catch his father-in-law in the act. Mildred insisted, however, that they leave well enough alone and not try to get a glimpse of her father and hero. She was afraid that efforts to see him might chase him off, and that was the last thing in the world she wanted.

Mildred was thrilled to be free of that severe pain, pain that had drug her down into despair. She had to put up with the normal aches and pains that come with advancing years as she became older. But she could handle that. And, she could handle smelling like a combination of a pile of harness and a freshly rained-on raspberry patch.

Wrong Words

Lots of fellows have gone to lots of extremes to get the girl of their dreams to marry them. Probably half of our history is history that happened as a direct result of just that.

A paradox is that when these extremes pay off and the guy gets the girl, he will find it difficult to remember their anniversary. There has to be some explanation for all that. Maybe, for some fellows, it's more fun to chase a girl than it is to catch her.

Whatever the explanation for all that, young Delany Erin had a bad case of it for Robin Dullus back in Mt. Carmel, Illinois, in the middle 1920s. He would have moved heaven and earth to get Robin to marry him. For a good five-year period of time, Erin simply wouldn't let go. He loved that Robin so much it hurt him right between the shoulder blades.

It wasn't as if Robin found it necessary to make a choice between Delany and someone else. She not only didn't love him, she didn't even particularly like the fellow. Robin never dated Delany, never had any interest in dating him and considered him to be something of a pest.

You wouldn't think that a guy would fritter away five full years of his life chasing a girl who had no interest whatsoever in him, and never gave him reason to think that she ever would. She thought that he really had the nerve to talk about marriage when they hadn't even gotten to the dating stage, and weren't about to.

Robin went with a number of different fellows there around Mt. Carmel, and finally married one of them in 1931.

Delany made one or two gestures through the years that led Robin to know that he still loved her. And, unfortunately for Delany, Robin's husband, Jake Hamilton, knew of Delany's continued interest in his wife.

A couple of times, Jake caught Delany out on the street and rearranged his hair for him...and his clothes and the bruises on his face. Jake had little time for Delany, just enough to dust him up real good now and then.

While that sort of dusting-offs now and then got the message through to Delany that he best not mess with Jake or Robin, it only made the man fear for his life, not change it. It was common knowledge in the community that Delany never had really given up in his pursuit of Robin. He just knew better than to do anything about it.

Delany never did marry. He was a bachelor his entire life, all the way to his death in 1972. Jake figured he was shed of that pesky Delany, and he was. That is, he was until three years after Delany died, so did Robin.

Robin's death started a whole new chapter in that old Delany/Robin situation.

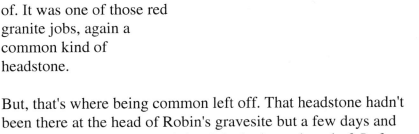

Jake had come up with a nice headstone for Robin, along with her dates of birth and death, the sort of headstone all of us have seen countless numbers of. It was one of those red granite jobs, again a common kind of headstone.

But, that's where being common left off. That headstone hadn't been there at the head of Robin's gravesite but a few days and the dangest thing happened that Jake had ever heard of. In fact, virtually nobody in the area had ever heard of such a thing.

A neighbor of Robin and Jake's saw the thing first and told Jake of how the name on that headstone no longer read ROBIN

HAMILTON. It was ROBIN ERIN. The dates of birth and death were still there, correctly, but it had Robin's name wrong.

Jake was angry that his neighbor would come up with such a bizarre story. He held back, but came close to telling that gal what he thought of her coming up with something like that.

He only allowed himself to express disbelief. He told her that there was no way such a thing could be.

Her insistence on the truthfulness of what she said finally led Jake to go out to the cemetery, just to put an end to that old biddy's gossip.

To say that Jake was surprised when he got there would not have done justice to the shock he felt when he looked at that headstone. There is was, big as life...ROBIN ERIN.

Jake gyrated between disbelief and anger as he stood there on the cinder path looking at that headstone. It couldn't be, but there it was!

The more Jake thought about it, the madder he got, and eventually worked himself into a state of fury, fury over someone having pulled such a tacky trick. Try as he would, he couldn't think of who in the community would do such a thing. Advancing years hadn't mellowed Jake any, and he was more than willing to take apart whoever had desecrated his wife's gravesite.

What really confused Jake, as well as others in the community, was that there was no evidence of that stone having been tampered with, no evidence that the letters had been filled in and then recut to show that name, ROBIN ERIN.

That confused Jake, others and the law. No one had an answer. Lots of folks knew that the stone certainly reflected the wishes of that Delany Erin, but he had been dead for a full three years, and there was no way that he could be doing that.

That is, there was no way that could be going on unless a person considered the possibility of Delany's ghost being the culprit. And there were any number of people in the community ready and willing to think exactly that. Jake wouldn't accept such an unlikely possibility. All he could do was get mad and order a new stone, one telling the truth as to the name of the person lying under the sod there in that cemetery.

It was a costly move, and one from which Jake got no particular positive satisfaction, other than to right a wrong. So a brand new headstone got hauled to the ditch and an even newer one took its place.

Like in most small towns, Memorial Day was an important day in Mt. Carmel, and the cemetery got all spiffied up for the occasion. There would be a lot of visitors on that day, and the cemetery association wanted to put its best foot forward as it did every Memorial Day.

The fence got painted for the occasion, the place got an especially diligent mowing and the flower beds got shaped up for the event.

Everything was in apple pie order......except for that gravesite of Robin Hamilton's. There, right out for everyone to see was apparently the same gravestone that had been there the day before, but reading ROBIN ERIN.

By this time, the idea of that first go-around being the work of the ghost of Delany Erin had gained currency in the community, and even Jake would no longer deny that possibility.

Jake's temper flared up again, but what can you do about the work of a ghost? Delany had ended up buried somewhere else, Jake neither knowing or caring. Jake couldn't even take it out on his adversary's own gravesite. He could just steam and get all het up thinking about his problem.

The solution of the problem turned out to be pretty simple. Jake had that second offending stone dug up and discarded. He replaced it simply by having the cemetery people sod over the spot so it eventually became indistinguishable from the surrounding grass.

That seemed to do the trick. If it was Delany's ghost doing that mischief, he gave it up.

Still Racing

The Youell family lived just off of 136, just east of Danville, Illinois, back in the 1980s and nearly 1990s.

Henry and Rita Youell had several children, and found their home out there in the country to be a fine place to raise kids. They were close enough to Danville that they could get there in just a few minutes to do the countless things that rural people have to do when they "go to town."

Yet, they were far enough removed from town that it wasn't somewhere that the kids could walk to or even ride their horses to. For the Youell family, the kids not being able to get to town on their own was simply a great way for them not to get into trouble.

So, what with the Youell home being home to a passel of active kids, there were any number of pets and horses for the kids to play with. They had swings, a teeter-totter and the creek to play in. All in all, it was a good deal for everyone involved.

While all the kids had their own horses, it was Terry who virtually lived on his. Terry and Windy were all but inseparable. Terry had named his horse Windy while the critter was yet a colt. He had great visions of his horse growing up to be a horse that was as fast as the wind.

We don't know, of course, if that hayburner's name had anything to do with that or not. But Windy proved to be one running horse. Maybe it would have been that way even if named "Slowpoke," but the only thing that Windy liked better than Terry was to run.

So, Windy and Terry tore up and down the road, whizzed around out in the pasture and raced up and down the creek. At the height of their fun, Terry was twelve years old and Windy was three years his senior.

It was in that twelfth year of Terry's that he died. It was some sort of ailment that didn't promise that sort of tragic end, but that's what happened.

While the other kids would offer to ride Windy from time to time, they were wasting their efforts. Windy was Terry's horse, and he wasn't about to let any of the other children get astride him.

Windy failed to come back from the pasture one day, prompting Henry to go out hunting him. He found the horse. It had apparently just laid down and died.

Henry and Rita figured that after they got that horse buried, that'd be the end of it. But they couldn't get out of their minds those golden years when their son and his horse Windy would tear up and down the place, racing to some point, only to race back at full tilt.

It occurred to the couple that what they should do is to take advantage of a local artisan's services wherein he would cast a statue of people's pets in brass. This fellow could take a few photos of the pet and recreate the thing in brass and could be used as a memento on a coffee table or wherever.

While most of the animals that this fellow would recreate were cats or dogs, he agreed to take on the project of doing a brass version of Windy. Starting with some photos the family had, and the saddle and the saddle blanket, the fellow made a brass version of that horse, complete with the gear that Terry had used with the animal.

The whole thing ended up being pretty pricey, but the family had a beautiful brass version of that horse. It provided them with comfort, being able to look over there on the end table and being able to see Windy standing there, just like he used to stand waiting for Terry to come home from school, so they could play.

The bridle was expertly done, with the reins casually draped over the saddle horn, and the saddle blanket on the horse's back, with the saddle placed squarely on it, just like Terry would always have it so placed.

Several times in the ensuing years, the family, or individuals within the family would hear a very muffled sound of a horse galloping in the night. Since the house was near the road, it struck them that someone was outside riding at night for some reason.

So, not a whole lot of attention was paid to that galloping noise. One night, however, Rita had gotten up to go to the bathroom, and could have sworn she saw a flash of a brassy-like color flash in the nightlight as it seemed to move swiftly from the living room into the dining room.

Rita did mention that the next morning, but dismissed it as being her imagination due to poor lighting and her sleepiness.

And, when one of the little kids told of seeing Windy galloping across the carpeted floor there in the living room one night, that was dismissed as being a little kid's overactive imagination.

The day the Youells realized their home was playing host to some nighttime racing around by a little brass horse was the day one of the kids, sitting there on the couch by that end table noticed something that could not be. She noticed that the saddle blanket on that statue of Windy was askew, askew as Windy's saddle blanket would always become after a running session.

The girl drawing everyone's attention to that is what made the Youells realize they had a real unique situation there in their house. That brass horse was in the practice of racing around the house, thus making those muffled sounds of hooves beating on a thick carpet instead of a dirt road.

That horse, saddle and saddle blanket was all cast in one hunk, only the bridle had been added later. It was leather as opposed to the brass. There is no way that saddle blanket could have slipped to cause it to be out of square there on that horse, and under the saddle, but there it was.

The Youells talked and talked about it to try to figure out what to do about the situation, and came to the conclusion that there was nothing they could do.

They couldn't straighten that blanket under the saddle since the horse, saddle and blanket was all one piece of brass. Not only could they not straighten it, but there was no way it could have gotten out of square in the first place. That is, there was no way unless the ghost of that horse would take over that hunk of brass after everyone had gone to bed. Apparently, ghosts can do anything.

The Youells left that statue of Windy there on that end table, and put up with the faint sounds of a racing horse a number of evenings.

One wonders, of course, if that horse had a twelve-year-old rider in his adventures around the house at night. Maybe so, maybe not.

Flingin' Mud

Leon and Holly Greene needed a place to live for only three months while the crew finished up their new house. This young couple had worked long and hard to get the money together to buy that lot and to come up with the down payment to build their dream home there on a little rise overlooking the Wabash.

They had found their little rental house had been sold out from under them, so all they needed was a place for only three months. After those three months, they knew they'd be able to move into their own house.

Holly's father, Brad Cantwell came up with what sounded like a great idea. He suggested that his daughter and Leon move out to the family cabin. That old cabin was kind of primitive, but it would work on a temporary basis.

The Cantwell cabin was one of three or four cabins down along the Wabash and east of Carmi, Illinois, and would be more than adequate for a short term living arrangement.

The more Leon and Holly talked about it there at that Sunday dinner at her folks, the more they liked the idea.

Of course, Holly's mother had to get all practical on them and remind everybody about that road back to those cabins.

"You guys don't call that road 'The Swamp' for nothing. All a thoroughly pregnant lady needs to do is to live out on the end of a road that had rightfully earned that name.

"You know as well as I do that thing can turn into an impossible mess if we get much rain."

Holly wasn't about to have any damp water thrown on her dad's good idea. She explained to her mother that the 'bad road' issue wasn't even an issue. She reminded her mother of her due date, and how they'd be tucked away safely in their new home by the time the baby came.

"Sure, honey, and there's never been a baby that ever came early. They are right on time, don't you know."

It was at that point that Leon interjected his two cents' worth.

"I didn't pay all that extra money for my 4-wheel drive for nothing. That new pickup with that 4-wheel drive would make short work of 'The Swamp.'

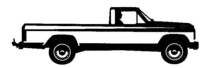

"All I'd have to do is pitch your daughter in that pickup and drop 'er down in 4-wheel and we'd make it out, I know we would. Besides that, like Holly said, we'll be out of there and in the new house by then."

Holly's mother had to admit that she had forgotten about how Leon's new truck was a 4-wheel drive. And she shared the commonly held opinion that Leon could work magic in driving into and out of the most impossible places with a pickup truck.

So, with the issue of "The Swamp" set aside, plans were made for the young couple to move on out to the cabin for those three months.

Those months went quickly out there at the cabin. Both Leon and Holly enjoyed those few weeks, but were still anxious for their move to their own brand new house.

It was at breakfast that Holly mentioned how they had only four more days there in the cabin and they'd be moving again, hopefully for the last time.

Holly's dad was going to help make the move that coming Saturday, so things were getting pretty exciting.

Holly's mom had planned to help too, of course, but came down with some sort of ailment and was sicker than sick, so she knew she wouldn't be able to help.

That Tuesday was the beginning of what turned out to be a really bad rainy spell. It was right after breakfast when the rain started, and it wouldn't let go.

The rain was a minor inconvenience compared to what else was going on. What had been foreseen to be just a spell turned out to be a really, really serious illness, and by that night, Mrs. Cantwell was gone.

The death of Mrs. Cantwell put a number of different things on hold, and certainly ended any plans for Leon and Holly to move that weekend.

The pair had gone to town because of all that had to be done in getting ready for the funeral. By Wednesday, the rains seemed to be just hitting their stride and things were really getting soggy. That conversation about "The Swamp" was recalled as the couple went back and forth between town and the cabin.

The Swamp didn't hold Leon up though, what with his fancy 4-wheel drive, but it got to be something of a rough ride.

What with losing her mother and having to fight that road, Holly wondered if there was anything else that could go wrong.

There was. There was, big time.

The couple had planned to go on into town Thursday for the funeral at about ten in the morning, but Holly's baby had other plans. It was just past dawn that day when it was obvious that the baby was gong to be born yet that morning. Instead of going to a funeral, it was time to go to the hospital.

Leon raised the whole neighborhood out there at the cabin site, getting help. He had to get Holly out to the truck and take off. He roused his neighbor lady to come along, and he woke up the other neighbor to come over to do his chores since he had to get out of there as soon as possible.

Fortunately, Leon's new truck had a crew cab, so the neighbor lady squeezed in there, Leon sat in the passenger's seat holding Holly and the neighbor was going to do the driving.

Off they went...at least they went as far as it took to get turned around so they could point the truck down the road to town. It was then that the truck let out with an ominous sound from the transmission and nothing worked. They could go neither forward or back.

There they sat, but with a pickup setting right alongside of them. It was the truck that belonged to the neighbor's fishing buddy. Immediately, the four of them piled out of Leon's truck and got into the other one sitting there.

The keys were in the truck, so the neighbor lost no time in getting that thing heading off for town.

This neighbor didn't enjoy the reputation for being able to make a pickup sit up and do tricks like Leon did, but he apparently rose to the occasion. By now the Swamp was strutting its stuff, looking a lot more like a shallow lake than it did a road.

Another neighbor and his wife came out into the yard to see what all the racket was about and watched those four roaring by. Those people later told about how that truck took off, clawin' and scratchin'. They told of how that truck just more than roared and spit fire as it ripped its way out of that area. They told of how those front wheels were grabbin' and clawin' at some hedge tree roots in an effort to get over those roots, frantically pulling that truck along. Those wheels in the back were obscured by a cloud of smoke and mud as they did their thing.

Leon, holding Holly in his arms, grinned over to the driver, thinking about how nice it was they had 'em a good modern truck, one that put the ol' Swamp in its place.

Up there on the highway, that truck threw globs of mud over oncoming cars as the foursome rushed to the hospital.

They got there, and got there in time. It was all kind of iffy there those last few moments, but they made it. They didn't make it all the way to the room. Their new little boy was born on the mobile bed as they rushed down the hall.

Meanwhile the family was faced with the need to go ahead with the funeral, go ahead without Mrs. Cantwell's daughter, as well as Leon.

One of the first things to do in preparation for the service was to open the casket for the traditional viewing.

The director of the funeral home found himself getting real impatient when his assistant got that casket lid part way up and then, for some reason or other, just held it part way up, looking down into the casket.

The director hurried over to get his helper moving. In fact, with poorly hidden impatience, the man grabbed hold of the edge of that lid and raised it on up himself. That is, he started to, but found himself, along with his assistant, holding the lid part way open, staring down into the casket.

There, lying in the casket, just as the director had left her, was Mrs. Cantwell. She was properly laid out, properly dressed and had the Bible clutched in her hands on her chest. There was the brooch she was to carry to the grave, and her glasses on her head.

There were also those little globs of mud on the lenses of her glasses. The director, like his assistant, stood there transfixed by the presence of those globs of mud on the lady's glasses.

Roused out of their inaction by the onset of organ music, the director took a handkerchief from his pocket and wiped the lenses clean.

After that the pair of them retired to the room behind the curtain so they could ask each other how such a thing could be.

It had been an eventful day, filled with a funeral, the escape out through The Swamp and the surprise birth of the new baby.

It was back at the cabin site where Leon's neighbor was explaining to his fishing buddy why they had taken off with the man's truck that morning. He explained that they had taken off with his truck since Leon's pickup chose that time to stop on 'em.

"But you couldn't have taken my truck."

"Yeah we did, and got it filthy dirty in the process. I'll run 'er through the car wash. It looks like a pig in a mud hole right now."

"But you couldn't have taken my truck. That'd be impossible."

"'Fraid not, buddy, we took 'er and made a real mess out of it. I'll run 'er through the car wash. I don't 'spose I can hold a candle to Leon when it comes to making a pickup set up and take notice, but I'll have to admit, I did perty well in stringin' 'er down through the Swamp!"

"I don't know what's going on here. I can see my truck is gone, but there's no way in the world you drove down through the swamp with my truck."

"Well, we did."

"You couldn't have. The road would be a real challenge for any 4-wheel drive, but I don't have a 4-wheel drive, mine's two."

Just how did those people make it down that road that day? How did the front wheels on that two-wheel drive go through all that clawin' and grabbin' at the roots of that hedge tree?

And how did that mud get splattered up on the glasses of Mrs. Cantwell when she was safely tucked away in that casket that day?

Eight-Twenty

While it was the common opinion in the community that the clock had been dropped rather than fell by accident, Gregory went free.

Well, almost free. No sooner did he get home again than a problem developed. It was his 8:20 problem. Regardless of the time of day, when Gregory Wyman looked at a clock or watch, it'd read 8:20. If it was two o'clock in the afternoon or toward midnight, any clock he'd look at would tell Gregory that it was 8:20.

When the noon whistle there in Attica blew, the fellows down at the lunch counter at the diner or in the office of the elevator would glance up at a clock, comment about the noon whistle and make whatever adjustments were necessary on their watches so the watches would agree with the whistle.

But Gregory didn't go through that little routine. He would studiously avoid glancing up at the clock on the wall. He'd avoid glancing at the watch belonging to the guy on the next stool. He wouldn't join in on the conversation about the noon whistle having just blown. He knew that any clock he looked at would tell him the time, of course. It'd tell him it was 8:20, the time of his wife's death.

Gregory had made the mistake of telling a couple of the other fellows about his telling time problem. News of that situation spread around town in about a nanosecond, and that simply confirmed the prevailing opinions that Gregory was guilty of the murder of his wife. People reasoned that his telling time problem was the work of the ghost of his wife, hassling him about his having murdered her.

It was on the first anniversary of the death of Frances that Gregory paid the ultimate price for his misdeed. It was on that evening that the Wyman house burned to the ground, costing Gregory his life.

It was almost midnight when the neighbors noticed the house to be on fire and called the fire department.

The fire department saved the foundation, but that was all they saved. The house was a total loss. Gregory's body was found in the bedroom, burned almost beyond recognition.

The ensuing investigation failed to lead to an understanding as to why both the window in the bedroom and the door were jammed shut...........jammed shut from the outside. That certainly aroused the curiosity of the sheriff, but nothing ever came of the further investigation.

But a lot of folks in Attica figured out pretty quickly who had done that. They laid responsibility for that little detail, as well as the fire itself, directly on the shoulders of the ghost of Frances Wymann.

That assumption tended to be confirmed by an interesting fact..........the fact that every clock in the house after the fire read 8:20.

The house is gone now, of course, as well as the foundation and the plants in the yard. It is simply a vacant area, indistinguishable from a couple of neighboring vacant lots.

There have never been any reports through the years of any other ghostly carryings on there on that vacant lot. Apparently, Frances got her licks in and let it go at that.

The Party Animals

Betty Howe and Jeff Waters were both known here in their hometown of Bluffton, Indiana, to be the type of people who tended to do things with a lot of fanfare and flamboyance. Both of them would tend to paint things with a wide brush.

So, when those two got married, no one was a bit surprised when they had a wedding that was a knock-your-socks-off wedding. They went all out in celebrating their union.

Given the nature of those two, it was joked among those in the community that they would probably come up with at least half a dozen kids in their first year of marriage.

Well, that didn't happen. In fact, half a dozen years went by with no little Waters there in their home.

The couple had wanted children and were about to conclude that they weren't going to have any. All that changed in the seventh year of their marriage and Betty wound up expecting.

In due time, little Dennis Waters joined the pair.

A year later was the first birthday for little Dennis, so a party was planned to celebrate the event.

And, of course, as was typical of that pair, it was to be a birthday party with all the stops pulled out. It wasn't going to be a wussy and timid little birthday party. It was going to be an all out party. They weren't going to be content with a few aunts and uncles, with a couple of neighboring kids and a small covey of grandparents.

They had all that of course, but also every neighbor within hailing distance, the mailman, some folks from the church and friends of both Betty and Jeff.

Even the babysitter and her boyfriend were there for that big first birthday.

Fortunately, the Waters had purchased, and moved into, a huge rambling old house, one of those houses with lots of history and hidden corners tucked away here and there. There was plenty of room in that old house for what proved to be a noisy and rambunctious birthday party. After all, you are only one once.

A couple of times during the course of the celebration, guests had approached Betty or Jeff to tell them about their having caught fleeting glimpses of what these people had thought were ghosts.

One fellow, especially, was adamant about having seen a figure up at the top of the stairway to the second floor. This guest

reported that the fellow was swaying a little back and forth, as if he was keeping time to the music out on the front porch.

This thing that impressed the guest about that fellow at the top of the stairs was that you could see the window behind him..........see right through the guy!

Betty and Jeff dismissed all that as a product of an overactive imagination on the part of their guest. They had never encountered any evidence of a ghost in that house, and were sure they didn't have one attending that birthday party.

Another of the guests, a gal who had been dancing out on the front porch where the Waters had a small band doing its thing, told them about what she experienced out there.

She told of how this fellow, a stranger, had asked her to dance and she had accepted.

She told of how, when the music stopped, her new acquaintance simply turned and walked through the door into the house. It seems the fellow didn't walk through the doorway, but through the door.

While all this was certainly interesting to the host and hostess, their duties that day kept them busy enough that they didn't really have the time to think very much about those reports of ghosts in their home.

During the next few months, others of the guests at that birthday party shared experiences they had had on that day, experiences that suggested that there might well have been some spooks at that event.

Since neither Betty nor Jeff had seen any evidence of any spooks during that party or afterward, they tended to politely listen, then dismiss such accounts.

The months went by with the Waters finding the nearing of Dennis' second birthday.

They decided they'd have another birthday party and this was going to be a humdinger. After all, you are only two years old just once, you know.

But the party didn't happen. The star attraction of the event fell out of a tree and ended up in the hospital on the day of his second birthday, getting his arm set and a cast put in place.

The Waters considered going ahead with a party, but then decided against it. They had their son in the hospital to worry about as well as their jobs, so scratched the whole birthday party idea for that second birthday.

But, apparently, they weren't the only ones who had plans for a party that day. It seems that the previous year's party had unleashed the inner party animals in the ghosts in that house.

It all started out with some dance music coming into the house from out on the front porch, music much like they had had a year ago that date.

Jeff stepped out onto the porch to investigate. After all, unexplained music from one's front porch isn't something you can ignore.

Just as Jeff opened the door to step outside, the music stopped. He caught only a half of a glimpse of a couple disappearing around the corner of the house. The only other evidence of any carryings-on out on the porch was the gentle swaying of the porch swing as if someone had recently gotten up and vacated it.

The movement of that porch swing on that day without even a breeze was sort of confusing to Jeff as he stood there, trying to figure out what was going on.

Even as Jeff was standing out there scratching his head, Betty was poking her head through the door from the dining room to the kitchen, trying to figure out what was with that noise coming from her kitchen. She had heard voices out there. They seemed to be voices associated with a party of some kind.

The only thing that greeted Betty when she peeked into the kitchen was the smell of some goodies. It smelled just like the goodies she had prepared for that party a year previous.

The two of them talked about those two situations and agreed that it certainly appeared as if a party must have been going on in their home. They recalled those reports of spooks from that affair of a year earlier and wondered if they might have some ghosts in their house after all.

But a slightly swinging porch swing and the unexplained aroma of goodies from out in the kitchen hardly proved anything, so they pretty much put all that out of their minds.

That is, they did until that evening when it was time to go to bed.

The two of them climbed those stairs together, making plans to go to the hospital the first thing in the morning to see how Dennis was doing.

Their talk about that hospital visit came to an abrupt halt when they got to the top of the stairs.

There, scattered from one end of that hallway to the other were the hats, the whistles and the streamers that Betty had stored away in a box on the top shelf of a bedroom closet.

A couple of the streamers had been hooked onto the woodwork in that hallway to form a festive decoration on one wall. It had all the appearance of the aftermath of a party...........a party where no one had bothered to clean up the mess.

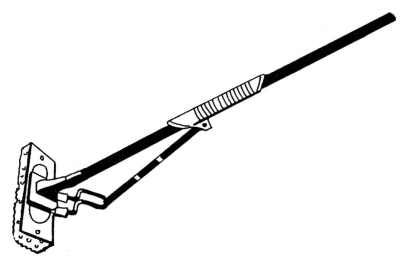

Incredulous over this turn of events, the couple took a bunch of photographs of that strewn-around mess in the hallway, then cleaned it all up. The couple still has those photos. They let the writer of this story examine the photos, but wouldn't agree to their being included in this book.

The Waters came to the conclusion that they not only had ghosts in their house, but that the party of a year earlier had unleashed the party instincts of those ghosts, and they were going to have one of their own.

Half hoping it'd work, and half hoping that it wouldn't, the Waters got all cocked and primed for Dennis' third birthday a year later. It was going to be another all-out party, but this third year was going to see a couple of changes. They had set up tape recorders and cameras. If they were going to have to have ghosts in their home, they wanted evidence of it.

Three of the guests at that party to celebrate Dennis' third birthday were professional ghost busters. They had drug in their own equipment that was supposed to pick up on the presence of ghosts.

It turned out to be a great party that third year...but that's all it was. No one shared a dance with a spook and nobody walked in through unopened doors. Nobody stood at the top of the stairs with a transparent body or otherwise.

Maybe those ghosts kind of got into the spirit of the thing, then lost interest in it all.

In the ensuing years, the family did run across evidence of a ghost from time to time, but apparently the days of the parties were over.

Betty and Jeff did agree, however, that it was fun while it lasted.

A String of Words

We are all products of our times. We all reflect, to some extent and in some ways, the forces in our societies that are not of our own making.

So it was with Rudie and Florence Lather of Portland, Indiana, just west of Ft. Recovery, Ohio, back in the early and mid 1900s.

Rudie subscribed to the notion that the man in the family was the one to make the major decisions and the woman's job was to work within that framework.

And, of course, among the major decisions that Rudie had to make were the various ones dealing with money arrangements.

Rudie's strategy was pretty straightforward. He was of the "in the mattress" school of thought. This couple had survived the Great Depression and Rudie was done with banks. He figured that banks were simply good places to lose one's savings, and he'd have no part of 'em, thank you.

For Rudie, "in the mattress" was simply a figure of speech. He didn't actually put his money in the mattress. He had a better hiding place than that. He figured that his hiding place was so clever and so good that the Lather savings was safe from thieves, fire, floods or anything else that ill-fortune could burden them with.

The thing that made Florence a bit uncomfortable was that Rudie wouldn't tell her where it was. If that economic turbulence they had lived through taught Rudie anything, it was that one couldn't be too careful in keeping such things secret.

So, he wouldn't tell her. Rudie had no intentions of doing Florence out of her rightful claim to that money. He was simply afraid that she might spill the beans someday, somehow, and that would be the end of their little nest egg.

"You might doze off at one of your Ladies Aid meetings and talk in your sleep. You might reveal where that money is, and not even know you do it."

The idea of dozing off during one of those Ladies Aid meetings was met with snorts of disbelief that Rudie would come up with such an idea, but that didn't do any good. He wasn't going to tell her, and that was that!

Florence's entreaties were to no avail. Her concerns that he might die before her and take the secret of the location of that money to the grave with him got her nowhere. Rudie Lather was healthy as a horse and wasn't going to be going around dying at any time in the near future.

He felt that he could divulge the location of that money in good time............maybe when they got old and grey.

Rudie Lather was a writer. He made his living by writing. He wrote columns for a number of newspapers. For most of these newspapers, it was on a weekly basis, so he'd have to come up with a column of the prescribed length each week for each of those newspapers.

Rudie was good at what he did and was able to provide a rather comfortable living for he and Florence. It was a good job. He could set his own hours and take a couple days off when the mood would strike him.

Rudie was, in fact, in the practice of writing columns ahead of time, so when he wanted to take a couple weeks off, he had columns in reserve to send in so he could take those vacations from time to time.

Rudie was not only good at what he did, but he was prolific. He would sit down at his desk with his yellow pad and a handful of good sharp pencils and crank that stuff out seemingly without effort.

Come time for a break, Rudie would sharpen new points on his EAGLE #2 pencils and be ready for a couple more hours of writing.

Often times people would comment about how Rudie did his work, seemingly without much effort, and ending up just as rested and refreshed at the end of the day as he was at the beginning.

That sort of cushy job was a rare sort of thing back when Rudie was doing his thing, rare enough that people would remark at how great it was that Rudie would find that work to be so easy.

Rudie's whimsical reply was always something to the effect that all the words he needed to use were simply there in his pencil, and it was just a matter of letting them string out there on the paper.

Rudie compared his work to that of a fellow who would sit down to carve an elephant out of wood. He'd tell that all the fellow had to do was cut away any wood that didn't look like an elephant. It was that simple. If you cut away all the wood that doesn't look like an elephant, you end up with a carved elephant.

"It's like that with my writing. All I have to do is to push that pencil around and all those words stored up there in the lead of my pencil simply comes out onto the paper, giving me a long line of words, just as if in a string."

Rudie even used that idea in his work. His letterhead illustration was a pencil with words spilling out of the end of the lead, all in a line, like a long black string............a string of words.

No one but the little kids believed that, of course, but it made for a good line.

To Florence, of course, all that was just a lot of idle talk, the sort of thing her husband was good at. Maybe that was what made him such a prolific writer.

So went the years in the Lather home. Rudie did his "stringing together of words" and Florence did whatever an obedient wife did.

The whole system worked well for the couple, and they found life to be comfortable and secure.

There was always that nagging issue of Rudie's refusal to tell Florence where he kept the savings hidden, but that was simply something that Florence couldn't do anything about, so lived with it.

The couple never had children and found it easy to fall into comfortable little routines........routines that enabled each of them to do their things.

The couple had a large room at the back of the house overlooking a pleasant wooded area there between Portland, Indiana, and Fort Recovery, Ohio. That room was their refuge, the place where each could pursue their projects.

Rudie had his desk, his chair, his clutch of yellow pads and his handful of pencils there. At the other end of the room, Florence had her sewing basket and her knitting. The pair spent a lot of time in that room overlooking the woods outside.

It was at that desk where Rudie had spent so much of his life where he also met the Grim Reaper. Rudie was, indeed, as healthy as a horse............a horse with an undiagnosed case of heart trouble.

It was that heart trouble that caught up with Rudie one sunny afternoon and turned Florence's world upside-down.

One minute she had a husband and the next she was a widow.

The shock of the events of that day and the turmoil of getting a

funeral arranged crowded out all other thoughts from Florence's mind until shortly after the funeral when she had time to think about the consequences of Rudie's death.

It was then that the financial impact hit Florence. It was then that she realized, with a sinking heart, that they had gotten a good start on the getting-old-and-grey part, but he never had told her where their savings were hidden.

It was then that Florence started to make a mental list of where that money could be. To her dismay, that list seemed to go on without end. Their place there on the edge of town, along with the outbuildings, the woods and the pond all posed the reasonable likelihood of literally hundreds of hiding places for that money.

Florence continued with her sewing and her knitting, but her thoughts became increasingly dominated with her fretting and stewing about the likely locations of that money.

She realized that even her comfortable little spot down at her end of that room overlooking the woods was in jeopardy if she couldn't find that money. What little funds she had wasn't going to be enough to see her very long.

The thought of losing her home and having no place to go was just more than she could bear.

Often, during her sessions there at her sewing machine, she would glance down to the other end of the room, thinking of how much she missed Rudie, and how they had spent so many pleasant days in that room.

But, dreamy recollections got crowded out in the real world of approaching poverty, adding to her frustrations over her inability to find their savings.

Florence's efforts to look under countless rocks, peer down into many, many holes in trees and to dig around in the garden got her nowhere. There were simply too many places to look and she found herself with less and less energy to make the search.

Florence's days became dominated with her futile efforts to find that money, and her nights were simply sleepless sessions of worrying about what was going to become of her.

After about three weeks of this, Florence was giving the house a halfhearted dusting, getting rid of the worst of the dust that had built up since the funeral.

Her heart was not in the job and she was doing a less than thorough job of it.

It was that dusting job that led her to each piece of furniture in the house. Her lick-and-a-promise dusting was going to be even less thorough at Rudie's desk. She was not in the mood to linger there.

She picked up that pad and pencil with one hand and was making a pass under it to get that desktop dusted off when she saw the strangest thing.

Out of the end of that pencil was a piece of black thread.......a piece of black thread somehow coming right out of the lead of the pencil.

This odd thing caused Florence to study that a bit closer, and was really shocked when she saw that the thread wasn't simply coiled up in a pile there on the pad, but seemed to consist of the little curls and coils to form letters.

As she picked that up, she saw that was exactly what it was. It was a little thing that looked like thread, but formed a series of letters. In fact, those letters strung on out to form words. It was like that little illustration that Rudie had used at the end of each of his columns.......a long unbroken string of words.

This was exactly the sort of thing that Rudie had often spoken of in such a whimsical way, a string of words coming out of his pencil.

Florence's hands were almost too shaky to do the job, but she got that string-like thing straightened out so she could read the words formed by that string.

Lying against that yellow pad, the words were easy to read once Florence got them lined up.

There it was:

In the well? What was all that about? How could that string have gotten there, how did it appear to come out of that pencil? What was the possible meaning of such a thing?

Florence let out a little gasp of air. Could it be that this odd thing was the work of Rudie's ghost telling her where their saving was? She had obsessed about that so much of late that her thoughts easily turned to that.

Florence might have gotten a start on the old-and-grey part, but her rush to the outside of the house would have done justice to an eighteen-year-old.

With strength she didn't even know she had, Florence tore the cover off the well and peered down into the darkness of that well. Way down, a long ways from her, she could see a little circle of light as the surface of the water in there reflected the blue sky above.

Then she saw it. She saw a loose brick on the wall of that well, a brick just within inches of her hand as she peered down into that well.

It was with more than a small measure of nervousness that Florence pulled that brick away from the wall.

And, there it was. Behind that brick was a little cavity where a nice fat wad of hundred dollar bills was secured with a piece of wire, holding them all together.

Florence waited for a minute or two, waited for her hands to stop shaking before she reached in and pulled that wad of bills out from their hiding place.

Florence's prayers were answered and her worries were over. A wad of hundred dollar bills is a fair amount of money today, and was even more so half a century ago.

Florence knew that Rudie had come back to tell her about where the money was. He had used that whimsical little thing about how the words were all piled up in his pencil and all he had to do was to let 'em string out for his writing.

It's kind of like carving an elephant. All you have to do is cut away anything that doesn't look like an elephant and you're home free. And, as the words come streaming out of a pencil when you are writing about elephants, the job is easy. Just throw away any of 'em that don't talk about elephants.

The Inconvenience

When Ben and Alice bought that old brick house in Springfield, Ohio, they neither knew nor cared about the history of the place. All they knew was that the price was right, and it would make one heck of a nice B&B. Right there within sight of I-70, yet far enough away to escape the traffic noises certainly added to the attractiveness of the house.

It was a fixer-upper without a doubt, and would involve a lot of work to bring it up to a quality appropriate for a B&B. Still, they thought it was the opportunity of a lifetime.

So, this couple bought the old Victorian mansion, and started down the long road of repairing it and restoring its 1800's beauty.

Ok, I'm lying about this being appropriate for this book. The circumstances detailed in this story didn't happen near here at all. This story really comes to us from London, Kentucky, on I-75.

But, I'm putting this story in this book anyway because it's such a good one. What I'm depending on is that the reader won't read this little bitty print in this footnote...or if he does, that he'll forgive my transgression in putting this story in this book.

Thanks for your indulgence.

In order to save money, the couple decided to live in the place while they were doing the refurbishing. During the course of their work, they found out a bit of the history of the place as they would visit with the neighbors.

The fact that it had been a house of ill repute back in the 1800s didn't really make any difference to them. After almost a hundred years of the house having been a private residence, neither Ben nor Alice expected anyone to confuse their new place with a house of ill repute.

The work progressed slowly as it always does when you are trying to bootstrap a project.

And, of course, there were any number of times that problems arose that gave them second thoughts about the wisdom of doing the project.

It was Ben who was most easily discouraged by the setbacks they would encounter.........

.........Alice, on the other hand, was more inclined to take the long view, and to realize that when they got done with it, it would be a beautiful place, well worth the time and money to make it all happen.

During each of those times that Ben would question if they should continue, Alice would counter with her standard answer... "It'll all work out alright."

Ben could just about depend on hearing that... "It'll all work out alright" whenever he'd suggest they sell the place, and move on.

Then, one night, an event took place that changed everything. It was after a hard day's work that Ben had gone to bed early. He was bushed, and all he wanted to do was hit the sack and get some sleep.

He had just crawled into bed, fluffed his pillow up to his liking and closed his eyes.

Suddenly, as he laid there on his side ready to go to sleep, he felt someone get into bed with him. This sort of surprised Ben because Alice had, just a few minutes earlier, told him that she was going to stay up and put one more coat of varnish on some woodwork they were working on.

Besides that, Alice had a habit of getting into bed as if she were mad at it. Ben had often told her that she got into bed like a 70 pound keg of nails.

His bedmate there sure didn't get into bed that way. It was a matter of kind of gently sliding into bed.

As Ben laid there, about to question Alice why she decided to come to bed after all, the second surprise came along. That surprise was in the form of a warm and gentle puff of breath on the back of his neck.

Now, Ben had been married long enough to know that Alice gently easing into bed, and giving him a provocative puff on his neck was totally out of character for her.

He turned to face her, and found a.........nothing, nothing at all. He had the bed all to himself, no wife, and no warm breath on the back of his neck.

126

Ben marveled at how he could be dreaming such a thing, not two minutes after laying down. He decided that he was even more tired than he thought, and had gotten to sleep as soon as he got that pillow squared away.

Ben went on to sleep with no further ado.

And, the project of fixing that house up continued. Ben was convinced that it was a never-ending job, and they'd be staining woodwork and hanging wallpaper when they were old and grey. But, he never did come up with a rebuttal to "It'll all work out alright."

It was about two weeks later, and Ben went to bed early again. He wasn't dead tired this time like the last time he had crawled in the sack alone, but just thought he'd get to bed early, and get up early.

The same routine...the laying on his side and the punching around on the pillow until it felt just right.

This time Ben hadn't yet even closed his eyes, and again there was that gentle sliding into bed next to him, followed by a provocative warm breath on the back of his neck.

Wow, this was just like that dream he had a couple weeks earlier, except this time he was awake. Ben wondered why Alice had suddenly taken up behavior that was so out of character for her.

"What's with your sliding into bed that way, Honey? What happened to your hitting the sack like you're mad at it?"

No answer.

"Honey, what's with your sneaking into bed that way?"

Again, no answer.

Twice he had talked to her, and she hadn't answered either time, so he turned so he could see her.............No Alice.........no anybody.

This time Ben knew he had something on his hands other than simply dreaming. Something was going on that needed explanation.

Ben laid there a moment, studying the pillow next to him when the thought struck him that this might be the work of a ghost. Alice was alive and well, he could hear her rattling the dishes

128

out in the kitchen as she cleaned up after their supper. It couldn't be Alice's ghost 'cause she wouldn't have one.

It was at that moment that he put two and two together and came up with the theory that his bedmate, temporary as she was, was the ghost of one of those fallen doves who had inhabited the house almost a hundred years earlier.

Now, good lookin' honeys softly sliding into bed with a fellow and puffing warm breath on his neck is something of a cause for celebration, even if she is a ghost.

Ben contemplated the situation as he laid there, about as wide awake as one person could be. He came to the conclusion that this house was a good idea, even if it was a lot of work and expense.

Sometimes there are intangible rewards in taking on a project, don't you know.

So, it was off to sleep for Ben, thinking of this good looking raven-haired beauty that had crawled into bed with him. Okay, so he made up the raven-haired part, but sometimes you have to improvise, you know.

Ben developed a new concern. He was concerned about the possibility that his experience that resulted from him going to bed early was not going to be repeated. He need not have feared that. From that point on, that happened a number of times.

Ben didn't bother Alice with all that. She had a lot on her mind, and he didn't want to unduly concern her. Ben was very considerate that way.

But, he chose to tell his buddies about his ghostly visitor. Actually, it was more of a case of bragging to his buddies about that.

Alice noticed that her husband had fewer bouts of wishing they hadn't gotten started on the B&B project. She was glad he was finally coming to see that things will all work out alright.

You know how things are. A buddy will tell his wife things, then his wife will talk to Alice and next thing you know, Alice knows all about the warm-breathed Honey.

It took some tall talking on Ben's part of explaining all that. He put it in the context of a dream, and how he only dreamed all that stuff, and he was really getting tired of having that same old tired dream every once in a while.

Ben took the precaution of holding his hand behind his back and crossing his fingers. He recalled that was a sure fire way of making it perfectly OK to cancel out the moral problem of telling a lie. He remembered that from his childhood. Everybody knew it was OK to lie if you crossed your fingers while doing so.

Surprisingly enough, Alice bought that. Perhaps she had been sniffing too many varnish fumes and didn't realize that Ben was lying through his teeth. They weren't dreams at all, much less dreams that Ben had tired of.

So, Alice put all that behind her. Besides that, you can't blame a fellow for having bad dreams, even if they are dreams about a ghost of a red-headed Honey. Ben had no idea where the "red headed" part came from, but figured that one of his buddies got the story wrong.

In spite of Alice's steadfast nature, the problems of redoing a large old Victorian house started to wear thin for her. So, when they discovered a leak in the roof that would require some expensive repair work, she wondered if they ought to give it up.

"You know, Ben, maybe what we ought to do is sell this place. You've been saying that for a long time now, and I think that maybe you're right."

Oops, this was a development that Ben wasn't ready for, much less come up with an argument against. He knew it was going to take some fancy footwork on his part to jump over to the other side of this "leave" or "not leave" issue.

"Yeah, well, we need to think about that, of course."

It was the best response Ben could come up with since he didn't have time there at the kitchen table to do the fancy footwork he needed to in order to switch sides on that issue.

"After all, Ben, when folks are paying a good price to stay in our B&B, they sure aren't going to appreciate what feels like a little honey crawling in bed with them and puffing warm breath on the back of their necks."

"Oh, no, of course not," Ben replied, hoping that he sounded half way sincere.

Having what seemed like Ben's agreement, Alice went on about how guys sure wouldn't want that inconvenience after a day's driving behind them, and another day's driving ahead of them.

Ben couldn't help but to think to himself..."What an inconvenience! What an inconvenience!"

This story took an unexpected turn as Ben was telling it to me.

"So, did Alice ever catch on to you?"

I had learned earlier from Ben that Alice had passed away shortly after the two of them finished up their B&B project. So, I wondered if she had learned about their ghost before she died.

"No," Ben said, "She never learned the truth, but there is sort of a sequel to this whole story."

"What's that?" I asked.

"Well, it wasn't long after Alice left us that those visits took on a new twist. The new twist was that if I'd go to be early, on occasion, I'd feel someone get into bed beside me, but after I lost Alice, it wasn't a matter of sliding into bed. It was still a ghost 'cause she'd be gone when I turned over."

"How, then, was it different?" I asked.

"It was different because after I lost Alice, my bed partner would get into bed like a 70 pound keg of nails........just like she was mad at the bed."

GHOSTS OF INTERSTATE 90 Chicago to Boston   by D. Latham

GHOSTS of the *Whitewater Valley* by Chuck Grimes

GHOSTS of Interstate 74   by B. Carlson

GHOSTS of the Ohio Lakeshore Counties   by Karen Waltemire

GHOSTS of *Interstate 65*   by Joanna Foreman

GHOSTS of Interstate 25 by Bruce Carlson

GHOSTS of the Smoky Mountains by Larry Hillhouse

GHOSTS of the Illinois Canal System by David Youngquist

GHOSTS of the Niagara River   by Bruce Carlson

Ghosts of Little Bavaria   by Kishe Wallace

Shown above (at 85% of actual size) are the spines of other Quixote Press books of ghost stories. These are available at the retailer from whom this book was procured, or from our office at 1-800-571-2665 cost is $9.95 + $3.50 S/H.

GHOSTS of Lookout Mountain by Larry Hillhouse

GHOSTS of Interstate 77 by Bruce Carlson

GHOSTS of Interstate 94 by B. Carlson

GHOSTS of MICHIGAN'S U. P. by Chris Shanley-Dillman

GHOSTS of the FOX RIVER VALLEY by D. Latham

GHOSTS ALONG I-35 by B. Carlson

Ghostly Tales of Lake Huron by Roger H. Meyer

Ghost Stories by Kids, for Kids by some really great fifth graders

Ghosts of Door County Wisconsin by Geri Rider

Ghosts of the Ozarks B Carlson

Ghosts of US - 63 by Bruce Carlson

Ghosts of Lake Erie by Jo Lela Pope Kimber

GHOSTS OF DALLAS COUNTY by Lori Pielak

Ghosts of US - 66 by Michael McCarty & Connie Corcoran Wilson

Ghosts of the Appalachian Trail by Dr. Tirstan Perry

Ghosts of I-70 by B. Carlson

Ghosts of the Thousand Islands by Larry Hillhouse

Ghosts of US - 23 in Michigan by B. Carlson

Ghosts of Lake Superior by Enid Cleaves

GHOSTS OF THE IOWA GREAT LAKES by Bruce Carlson

Ghosts of the Amana Colonies by Lori Erickson

Ghosts of Lee County, Iowa by Bruce Carlson

The Best of the Mississippi River Ghosts by Bruce Carlson

Ghosts of Polk County Iowa by Tom Welch

Ghosts of Interstate 75 by Bruce Carlson

Ghosts of Lake Michigan by Ophelia Julien

Ghosts of I-10 by C. J. Mouser

GHOSTS OF INTERSTATE 55 by Bruce Carlson

Ghosts of US - 13, Wisconsin Dells to Superior by Bruce Carlson

Ghosts of I-80 by David Youngquist

Ghosts of Interstate 95 by Bruce Carlson

Ghosts of US 550 by Richard DeVore

Ghosts of Erie Canal by Tony Gerst

Ghosts of the Ohio River by Bruce Carlson

Ghosts of Warren County by Various Writers

Ghosts of I-71 Louisville, KY to Cleveland,OH   by Bruce Carlson

GHOSTS OF OHIO'S LAKE ERIE SHORES & ISLANDS VACATIONLAND by B. Carlson

Ghosts of Des Moines County   by Bruce Carlson

Ghosts of the Wabash River   by Bruce Carlson

Ghosts of Michigan's US 127   by Bruce Carlson

GHOSTS OF I-79   BY BRUCE CARLSON

My Very Own Notes

My Very Own Notes

My Very Own Notes

To Order Copies

Please send me _____ copies of
Ghosts of the Wabash River at $9.95
each plus $3.50 S/H. (Make checks
payable to Quixote Press.)

Name_____

Street_____

City _____ State _____ Zip_____

QUIXOTE PRESS
3544 Blakslee Street
Wever, IA 52658
1-800-571-2665

To Order Copies

Please send me _____ copies of
Ghosts of the Wabash River at $9.95
each plus $3.50 S/H. (Make checks
payable to Quixote Press.)

Name_____

Street_____

City _____ State _____ Zip_____

QUIXOTE PRESS
3544 Blakslee Street
Wever, IA 52658
1-800-571-2665